County Council

Libraries, books and more...........

RECEIVED

1 6 NOV 2015

W/TON LIBRARY

1 6 MAR 2017

2 3 AUG 2017

1 0 DEC 2015   - 8 OCT 2016

3 0 OCT 2018

2 5 FEB 2016   2 8 NOV 2016

0 8 SEP 2016   Boltongate Book Drop

1 2 APR 2022

Please return/renew this item by the last date shown.
Library items may also be renewed by phone 2023
030 33 33 1234 (24hours) or via our website
www.cumbria.gov.uk/libraries 1 1 JUL 2023

Cumbria Libraries

CLIC
Interactive Catalogue

Ask for a CLIC password

To Katie and Millie

Special thanks to
Rachel Elliot

ORCHARD BOOKS
Carmelite House, 50 Victoria Embankment, London EC4Y 0DZ.
Orchard Books Australia
Level 17/207 Kent Street, Sydney, NSW 2000
A Paperback Original

First published in 2015 by Orchard Books

HiT entertainment

A CIP catalogue record for this book is available
from the British Library.

ISBN 978 1 40833 953 4

1 3 5 7 9 10 8 6 4 2

Printed and bound by CPI Group (UK) Ltd, Croydon, CR0 4YY

MIX
Paper from
responsible sources
FSC® C104740

The paper and board used in this book are made from wood from responsible sources

Orchard Books is an imprint of Hachette Children's Group and published by
the Watts Publishing Group Limited, an Hachette UK company.

www.hachette.co.uk

Ariana
the Firefighter
Fairy

by Daisy Meadows

ORCHARD

www.rainbowmagic.co.uk

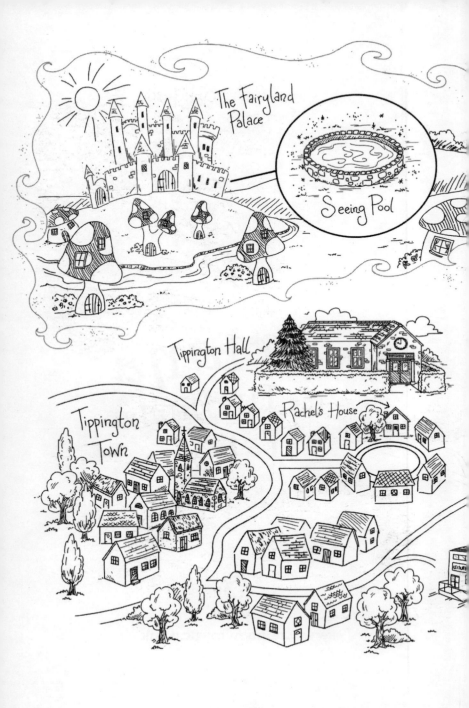

Jack Frost's Ice Castle

Aunt Lesley's Surgery

The Fire Station

Tippington Park

The Leisure Centre

Jack Frost's Spell

These silly helpful folk I see
Don't know they could be helping me.
But they will fail and I will smirk,
And let the goblins do the work.

I'll show this town I've got some nerve
And claim rewards that I deserve.
The prize on offer will be mine
And I will see the trophy shine!

Contents

Calamity Kitten

The kitchen was filled with the clatter of cups and plates and the smell of toast – the Walker family had just finished breakfast.

"It's another gorgeous spring day," said Rachel Walker, stepping out of her back door into the garden. "I'm so glad we don't have to sit inside a classroom today."

Her best friend, Kirsty Tate, followed her and took a deep breath of fresh air. She was staying with Rachel in Tippington for half term. The kitchen window opened and Mrs Walker leaned out to call to them.

"Girls, please would you water the

plants while you're out there?" she asked. "They need extra care in all this heat." It had been a wonderfully sunny half term so far.

Rachel and Kirsty filled their watering cans and started to water the beautiful plants. The spring bulbs were flowering and scenting the air.

Just as Kirsty was watering the tulips, she heard a faint sound. Rachel heard it too, and stopped beside the daffodils to listen.

"It's a meow," said Kirsty. "There must be a cat in the garden. Come on, let's find it!"

They put down their watering cans and searched among the bushy plants and behind the plant pots, but there was no sign of a cat. Then Bailey, the little boy who lived next door, popped his head over the fence. He looked worried.

"Rachel, please will you help me?" he called. "My kitten, Pushkin, has climbed on top of the shed in your garden, and now she's stuck!"

"Of course we will," said Rachel at once. "Don't worry, Bailey – we'll get her down."

They walked to the little green shed at the end of the garden, where the lawnmower and gardening tools were kept. On the roof, they could see a pair of large, scared eyes peeping down at them.

"Come on, puss," said Rachel in a gentle voice. "Don't be scared – you can get down."

Pushkin took a step back.

"Maybe she'll come down to eat something," said Kirsty thoughtfully. "Bailey, could you go and get some of her favourite food?"

Bailey nodded and disappeared from view. The tiny tabby kitten was letting out little meows and crouching flat against the roof.

She took a step closer to the edge of the roof and meowed again. Bailey's head popped back up, and he held out a dish of cat food over the fence.

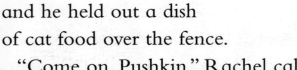

"Come on, Pushkin," Rachel called. "Look, it's your favourite. Time to come down."

She held out her hand, and Pushkin gazed at her for a long time. Then, just when it seemed as if she might stay on the roof forever, the little kitten plucked up her courage and jumped down onto the fence. For a moment she looked a little wobbly.

"You can do it, Pushkin," called Kirsty.

Pushkin leaped down into Bailey's garden. He let out a delighted cheer.

"Thank you, Rachel!" he called. "Thank you, Kirsty!"

"No problem," said Rachel, smiling at the little boy. "We're just glad she's safe."

"She loves climbing things," said Bailey with a grin. "She's always getting stuck, though."

The girls hung over the fence and watched as Pushkin ate her food. Then Bailey picked up the kitten and the dish, waved to the girls and headed back inside his house. Rachel and Kirsty smiled at each other.

"Aunt Lesley's right," said Rachel. "It's a great feeling to be able to help people."

"Helping Bailey and Pushkin was almost as good as helping the fairies," said Kirsty in a low, happy voice.

Rachel and Kirsty had often visited Fairyland, and they loved being able to help their magical friends when Jack

Frost caused trouble for them. Right now they were caught up in one of their biggest fairy adventures ever. Jack Frost had stolen the magical objects that belonged to the Helping Fairies, and the girls had promised to try to find them.

Rachel's Aunt Lesley was a doctor, and she had been nominated for the Tippington Helper of the Year Award. Yesterday, she had been acting very strangely until the girls had returned Martha the Doctor Fairy's magical watch to its rightful place. There were still three objects to find, and time was running out.

A Garden Visitor

The award ceremony was later that week, and the girls knew that if they hadn't found the magical objects by then, it would be a disaster.

The Tippington Helper of the Year Award was a local prize that was given to a special person in the community whose job it was to help others. Rachel's

Aunt Lesley was staying with the Walkers while some building work was being done on her house, so Rachel and Kirsty had heard all about her work and how much she enjoyed helping people.

"I almost wish we could tell Aunt Lesley about the Helping Fairies and Jack Frost," said Rachel as she went to the outside tap to fill up her watering can again.

"Stop!" cried Kirsty, as Rachel was reaching her hand out to the tap. "Your watering can is glowing!"

Hastily, Rachel put the watering can down and watched as the glow inside it grew brighter and brighter.

"Do you think it's a fairy?" she asked in excitement.

Kirsty nodded, too thrilled to speak. Seconds later, Ariana the Firefighter Fairy came fluttering out and perched on the spout. The girls remembered her from their meeting in Fairyland the day before.

"Good morning, girls!" she said in a bright voice. "I'm hoping that I can find my magical firefighter's helmet today. Will you help me?"

"Of course we will!" said Kirsty at once.

She and Rachel knew that without their magical objects, the Helping Fairies couldn't help everyday heroes like Aunt Lesley do their jobs. Jack Frost wanted to win the Tippington Helper of the Year Award himself, but he wasn't prepared to do any helping! Instead, he had sent

his mischievous goblins to do the jobs
of all the award nominees. He planned
to pretend that he had done all the jobs
himself so that he could win.

"I just don't know where to start
looking," said
Ariana, holding
out her arms.
"How are we ever
going to find the
goblins?"

"Don't give up,"
said Kirsty, smiling
at the little fairy. "We
got Martha's watch
back and now Rachel's
Aunt Lesley is helping her
patients again. We'll find your helmet
too."

"Yesterday, the goblins took Martha's magical watch to Aunt Lesley's surgery," said Rachel in a thoughtful voice. "I wonder if they could have taken your helmet to the fire station."

Kirsty looked anxious.

"The goblins could cause serious trouble at the fire station," she said. "We have to get the helmet back quickly, or the firefighters won't be able to do their jobs."

"I've got an idea," said Rachel. "Dad told me that there's an open day at the fire station today. Let's ask if we can go and look around. If

the goblins are there, I'm sure we'll see them. They're not very good at keeping out of sight!"

"That's a wonderful idea!" cried Ariana. "Let's go!"

Ariana whooshed through the air and dived into Kirsty's pocket to hide. Then the girls ran towards the house to find Mrs Walker. But when they burst through the back door into the kitchen, Mrs Walker was nowhere to be seen. Aunt Lesley was there, working on her computer at the kitchen table. She

looked up when Rachel called to her
mum.

"Your mum's popped out to the shops,"
she said. "She asked me to keep an
eye on you while I'm updating my
patient files."

"Oh no," groaned Rachel. "We were
hoping to go to the open day at the fire
station. Dad said that they're holding
demonstrations of firefighting."

Aunt Lesley closed her laptop.

"That sounds interesting," she said. "I've actually just finished my work – it didn't take as long as I expected. I'd be delighted to take you to the fire station, if you'd like to go with me instead?"

"That would be amazing!" said Kirsty. "Are you sure?"

"Of course!" said Aunt Lesley. "It'll be a chance to see my old friend Isobel, who works there. She's been nominated for the Tippington Helper of the Year Award too."

Kirsty and Rachel exchanged a knowing look. If Isobel was one of the nominees, then the goblins would probably be trying to take over her job. It was lucky that Aunt Lesley knew her and could introduce them.

"We'll go in my car," said Aunt Lesley. "I'll just write a note to tell your mum where we've gone."

A few minutes later, Kirsty and Rachel were sitting in the back of Aunt Lesley's car and they were zooming towards the fire station.

Fearful Firefighters

"Is Isobel a firefighter, Aunt Lesley?" Rachel asked.

"Yes," said Aunt Lesley. "Other people run away from fires, but she puts on her helmet and her equipment and runs into them."

"She must have a lot of courage," said Kirsty in awe.

"Isobel is the bravest person I know," said Aunt Lesley. "She has saved so many lives and helped so many people, I've lost count."

They arrived at the fire station and Aunt Lesley parked the car. There was a large crowd of people in the courtyard in front of the building.

"Look, there are lots of people here for the open day," said Rachel, clambering out of the car.

There was a pretend building in the middle of the courtyard.

"I expect they'll use that for the demonstrations later," said Aunt Lesley.

"But where are all the firefighters?" asked Kirsty, looking around.

There wasn't a single firefighter to be seen, even though it was past the start time for the open day.

"Let's go inside the fire station," said Aunt Lesley. "I want to show you something."

When they walked inside the building, the first thing they saw was a shiny silver pole that reached up through the ceiling.

"The firefighters slide down this pole when there's an emergency call," said Aunt Lesley. "It's here so they don't waste time running down the stairs, and they can get to the fire as quickly as possible."

"It's looks like fun," Kirsty whispered to Rachel.

Rachel grinned back at her.

"I wish we could have a go," she said.

They all looked up to the top of the fire pole and saw several worried faces staring down at them.

"Isobel!" exclaimed Aunt Lesley, sounding very surprised. "What are you doing up there? There are lots of people here for your open day. Come on down."

Rachel and Kirsty looked more closely and saw that all the people at the top of the pole were in uniform. They were all firefighters.

"We can't," said Isobel in a trembling voice. "It's too far."

"What do you mean?" asked Aunt Lesley, confused. "Just slide down the pole."

"Ooh, no, I couldn't," said Isobel. "I don't like heights."

"It makes me dizzy just thinking about it," squeaked a big, burly firefighter.

"I can't look," said another, squeezing his eyes shut.

"I can't understand it," said Aunt Lesley to the girls. "Is it some sort of joke?"

"I don't think they're joking," said Kirsty, exchanging a secret glance with Rachel.

They both knew exactly why the firefighters weren't feeling very brave. They wouldn't have the courage they needed to do their jobs until Ariana's magical helmet was back in Fairyland where it belonged.

Suddenly there was a deafening noise from the fire engine outside the fire station. Its siren blared and all its lights started flashing. Aunt Lesley barely seemed to notice the noise – she was too worried about her friend.

"I'm going up to see if I can help Isobel," she said.

She started up the stairs, and Kirsty and Rachel ran outside to see what was happening.

Four firefighters were climbing out of the
fire engine, swinging themselves down
like acrobats while the crowd cheered
and clapped.

"I've never seen firefighters in a green uniform before," said Rachel. "Even their boots are green."

"They must be goblins!" Kirsty whispered.

A Drenching Demonstration

When she heard what Kirsty said, Ariana peeped out of the pocket where she was hiding.

"You're right," she whispered to the girls. "Look at that plump goblin on the end. He's wearing my magical helmet!"

Each goblin was wearing a helmet with a large visor that covered his face. Three of the helmets were green, but the fourth was yellow and sparkling in the spring sunshine.

"We *have* to get that helmet back," said Rachel, squeezing her hands into fists. "Until it's returned to Fairyland, the real firefighters won't have any courage, and they won't be able to protect people."

"But how can we get the helmet back?" asked Ariana. "It just seems impossible."

"Nothing is impossible," Rachel replied. "We'll find a way!"

Just then, the plump goblin wearing Ariana's magical helmet grabbed a hose.

"Time for a demonstration!" he squawked.

He climbed up the ladder of the

practice building with a hose and
showered the other goblins
with water.

"Hey, stop it!"
screeched the
other goblins.
"You'll be
sorry!"

They
grabbed
hoses too,
and within
seconds they
had started
a massive
water fight.
Water
sprayed over the crowd and soaked
everyone, including Rachel and Kirsty.

People laughed at first, but after a few minutes they started to get annoyed.

"This isn't much of a demonstration!" said one man.

"There wasn't even a fire to put out," a lady grumbled.

"Stop!" shouted a young mother.

But the goblins took no notice until the loudspeaker in the courtyard let out a loud squeal.

"Emergency! Emergency! A kitten is stuck up a tree. Firefighters required! Hurry!"

The goblins flung down their hoses and raced to the fire engine.

"To the rescue!" bellowed the plump goblin.

With the siren wailing, the fire engine zigzagged towards the crowd, trailing its

hoses behind it. People scattered
as it lurched out of the courtyard,
turned sharply and hurtled off down the
road, with goblins hanging on to it for
dear life.

"How are we going to get the helmet
back now?" Kirsty asked.

"We need to follow the fire engine," said Rachel. "Ariana, can you turn us into fairies? The only way to catch up with those goblins is to fly after them!"

"Of course!" said Ariana. "But you'll need to hide somewhere so that I can transform you."

The girls looked around and Kirsty grabbed Rachel by the hand.

"The garage," she said. "It's empty now. Come on!"

They ran into the deserted fire engine garage, and Ariana flew out of Kirsty's pocket. She flourished her wand and a puff of fairy dust sprinkled down on the girls. They instantly shrank to fairy size.

"I love flying!" said Rachel, spinning into the air and scattering fairy dust from her fluttering wings.

Kirsty twirled up beside her, and Ariana joined them. For a moment, everything was forgotten except the joy of flying on glimmering fairy wings. Then Rachel clapped her hands together.

"Let's catch that fire engine!" she exclaimed.

Flying high so that they wouldn't be spotted, the fairies zoomed in the direction the fire engine had gone.

Luckily the goblins didn't know much
about driving a fire engine, and it was
slowly bucking along, only just staying
on the right side of the road.

"It's heading towards your house,
Rachel!" Kirsty cried.

With a squeal of brakes, the fire engine
stopped just before Rachel's home. Bailey
came running out of his house, looking
tearful.

"Thank you for
coming!" he called
to the goblin
firefighters. "My
kitten can't get
down!"

The goblins got
down from the fire
engine on wobbly legs.

"Where's the problem?" said the plump goblin in the magical helmet.

Bailey pointed at the tall oak tree that grew opposite his house.

"She's on a branch up there," he said. "Please help her."

The goblin puffed out his chest and started snapping out orders at the other goblins.

"Get a ladder! Put it up against the tree! Not like that, you idiot!"

"Who does he think he is, Jack Frost?" grumbled one of the other goblins as the fairies fluttered over their heads towards the tree.

The goblins were busy leaning the ladder against the trunk. Quickly, the fairies darted among the leaves and perched on the branch beside Pushkin. They were hidden from view, but they could hear every word the goblins were saying.

"Get out of my way," the tallest one said, elbowing the others aside. "The bravest should go first."

"In that case, it should be me," said a knock-kneed goblin.

"No, ME!" squawked a goblin with extra-big feet.

He shoved the other two to the

pavement and started to climb the ladder.

"Me next!" screeched the knock-kneed goblin.

"Me first!" exclaimed the one wearing the magical helmet, trying to pull the others down. "I'm the bravest of the lot of you!"

As the goblins squabbled, tears welled up in Bailey's eyes.

"I just want you to rescue my kitten," he pleaded.

Kirsty looked up at the kitten, who was gazing at the fairies in surprise.

"I don't think the goblins are going to help Pushkin," she said. "It's up to us."

A Goblin Pyramid

"Look, Pushkin," said Rachel, pointing to Bailey. "Time to go home."

Pushkin gave a longing little meow.

"All you have to do is make your way down, step by step," said Kirsty. "You can do it, Pushkin. Bailey wants to give you a cuddle."

Pushkin purred and took a cautious little jump to the next branch down.

"That's it!" said Ariana. "Good kitten. Keep going!"

As Pushkin made her way slowly down the tree, Rachel, Kirsty and Ariana kept praising her and telling her how well she was doing. As

the goblins squabbled on the ladder, the kitten grew more and more confident, until at last she reached the bottom of the tree and jumped into Bailey's arms. The three fairies cheered and clapped.

Bailey looked up at the bickering goblins, shook his head and carried Pushkin back into the house. The goblins were too busy arguing about who was bravest to notice that the kitten had gone. Now they were all on the ladder, and it was shaking as they pulled at each other.

"They're going to fall!" cried Ariana.

"Quickly, turn us back into humans," said Kirsty. "This might be our chance to get the helmet."

They all hid behind the tree and Ariana turned them back into humans with a wave of her wand. At the same time, the goblin wearing Ariana's helmet tried to climb over the others to get up the ladder first. Rachel and Kirsty darted out from behind the tree, but they weren't

quick enough. The ladder broke and the
goblins fell down.

As the goblins tumbled around on the
pavement, their helmets came off and
rolled into the gutter.

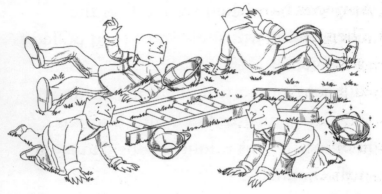

"Quick, grab my helmet!" called Ariana
from behind the tree.

But before the girls could reach it, the
plump goblin grabbed it and wedged
it back on his knobbly head. The girls
slipped back behind the tree before they
were spotted.

"We have to get that kitten," said the knock-kneed goblin. "If we don't, Jack Frost will say we haven't done the job!"

"Well how are we supposed to do that without a ladder, genius?" asked the plump goblin.

They still hadn't noticed that the kitten had already been rescued. They tried standing on each other's shoulders, with the goblin in the magical helmet on the bottom row. His hands were raised above his head, holding up the goblin on his shoulders.

"This is our chance," Rachel whispered. "While his arms are up, we can just lift the helmet off his head, and he won't be able to grab us."

She tiptoed out from behind the tree, but just then Pushkin raced out through her cat flap and scampered over to the pyramid of goblins. Her fluffy tail brushed against the goblins' feet and they squealed.

"That tickles!"

"Stop that!"

The pyramid collapsed in a heap of giggling goblins, and the helmet rolled off again.

58

But this time the goblin with the extra-
big feet picked it up and tucked it under
his arm.

"I'm in charge now," he shouted. "I'm
the boss because I've got the special
helmet. You all have to line up and look
smart – I'm going to inspect you."

Grumpily, the other goblins nudged
each other into a wonky row and stood
up as straight as they could. The goblin
with the magical helmet strutted up and
down in front of them, shaking his head
and tutting.

"Your buttons are not shiny enough!"
he told the knock-kneed goblin. "None
of you is wearing the right sort of
boots. Why aren't you carrying fire
extinguishers?"

"We're not allowed—"

"Silence!" he bellowed. "No answering back! Stand up straight!"

Rachel joined Kirsty behind the tree again.

"It's no good," she said. "They're just not letting go of it."

Kirsty watched Pushkin darting over towards the hoses in the fire engine, and then thought back to the water fight at the fire station.

"I think I've got an idea!" she said.

Help from
a Hose

Kirsty raced over to the fire engine
and grabbed one of the hoses, quickly
followed by Rachel.

"Turn it on!' cried Ariana, hovering
between them.

Rachel turned the wheel valve and
a huge, powerful jet of water shot out
of the hose so fast that it made the

girls stagger backwards. It took all
their strength to aim the water at the
pompous, big-footed goblin, who now
had the magical helmet on his head.

"Aim for the helmet!" Rachel
exclaimed.

The goblins shrieked as the ice-cold
water drenched them, and then the girls
hit their target. The helmet flew off
the goblin's head and Ariana swooped
through the air to catch it.

At once, the helmet shrank to fairy size. Rachel turned the hose off and she and Kirsty stood there, panting, as the goblins stared at them with open mouths.

"You can't take that!" wailed the goblin with the extra-big feet. "What are we going to tell Jack Frost?"

"He'll be ever so cross," said the knock-kneed goblin, starting to bite his fingernails.

"You don't always have to do all the naughty things he tells you to do," said Rachel.

"But we *like* being naughty," the tallest goblin said in a sad voice.

Kirsty couldn't help but feel a bit sorry for them. She whispered an idea to Ariana. The little fairy looked surprised, but she waved her wand and four toy fire engines appeared in front of the goblins, with real working pedals and padded seats. Instantly, the goblins' frowns were replaced with excited smiles and whoops of joy. They leaped into the fire engines and pedalled away down the street.

"Nee-naw, nee-naw!" they bellowed at top volume.

"They've forgotten all about Jack Frost," said Rachel with a grin.

"I wish I could do the same!" Ariana
sighed, but she was smiling. "Girls, thank
you so much for helping me to find my
magical helmet. I can't wait to show
the other Helping Fairies that we've got
another of our magical objects back."

"We'll find all of them, we promise,"
Kirsty replied.

With a last
wave, Ariana
disappeared back
to Fairyland and
the girls shared a
happy smile. Jack
Frost wasn't going
to find it as easy
as he had thought
to cause trouble
in Tippington!

A little later, the girls were back at the fire station and the open day was in full swing. Rachel and Kirsty had called Aunt Lesley and told her that they had found the missing fire engine. Isobel had come to pick it up, and the girls had fun riding in it and learning what the fire engine driver had to do.

The official demonstration was very interesting. The girls and Aunt Lesley watched and gasped with the rest of the spectators as Isobel led the other firefighters up a ladder to rescue a mannequin. They did it perfectly – with no water fights!

"Isobel's so brave," said Aunt Lesley. "I think she and the other firefighters were just playing a little joke on us earlier."

Rachel and Kirsty smiled and nodded,

but they also squeezed each other's hand, enjoying sharing their secret with each other. After the demonstration, they hurried over to congratulate Isobel.

"You were amazing," said Rachel.

"So brave," added Kirsty. "I hope I would be that brave if I saw a fire."

"Thank you for the compliment," said Isobel, "but the bravest and best thing you could do would be to call the fire brigade. It's part of our job to deal with fires and help people."

"And kittens up trees?" asked Rachel with a grin.

"Sometimes," said Isobel, laughing.

Rachel looked into the main building and saw the sunlight glinting on the shiny silver pole. She took a deep breath.

"Isobel," she said, feeling a little shy, "would it be possible to have a go at sliding down the pole? Just once?"

Isobel threw back her head and laughed.

"Of course," she said. "I should have asked if you wanted to try it – everyone always does!"

She gave the girls fire helmets to wear and led them up the stairs to the top of the pole.

"Now, don't be scared," she said. "I'll go first so you can see how it's done."

The girls watched Isobel carefully, and then Rachel zoomed down the pole with an excited squeal. Kirsty followed quickly, laughing as Isobel caught her at the bottom.

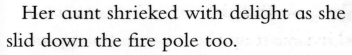

"That is so much fun!" she exclaimed.

"Try it, Aunt Lesley!" Rachel called up.

Her aunt shrieked with delight as she slid down the fire pole too.

"I think I might get one installed at the surgery," she joked. "It might help to cheer up my poorly patients!"

Still laughing, they all said goodbye to Isobel and promised to see her at the Tippington Helper of the Year Award ceremony.

As Aunt Lesley went to fetch the car, Rachel and Kirsty shared a happy smile.

"We've already got two of the Helping Fairies' magical objects back from Jack Frost," said Rachel. "Martha and Ariana must be glad that they can help people again."

"Yes, but Perrie and Lulu still need us," said Kirsty. "We have to find the siren and whistle before the ceremony."

"It feels even more important after today," said Rachel, looking around at all the smiling faces around her. "We have to make sure that community heroes like Isobel can carry on helping others."

"We will," said Kirsty. "We might not be able to fight fires, but I'd say we can definitely help the Helping Fairies – and I can't wait for the next adventure!"

Meet the Storybook Fairies

Can Rachel and Kirsty help get their new fairy friends' magical objects back from Jack Frost, before all their favourite stories are ruined?

www.rainbowmagicbooks.co.uk

**Now it's time for Kirsty and
Rachel to help...**

Perrie the Paramedic Fairy

Read on for a sneak peek...

"I've never seen the park so busy," said
Rachel Walker, gazing around.

It was a sunny spring morning, and
Tippington Park was packed with people.
Everyone was there to watch the start of
the Tippington Town Half Marathon.

"I hope your dad wins," said Rachel's
best friend, Kirsty Tate.

Kirsty was staying with Rachel for
the spring half-term holidays. They both
looked across to where Mr Walker was
warming up for the race. He was wearing
a white vest top and running trousers.
The number seven was pinned to his vest.

"He's in with a good chance," said Rachel. "He's been training every day for months! But he always says it's not about winning."

"It's about taking part," agreed Mrs Walker, who was standing behind them. "Your dad has already raised lots of money for charity."

The girls gazed around at the crowds of runners and spectators. Everyone looked happy and excited. The half-marathon was an important event for Tippington Town. People looked forward to it all year long.

"I wonder if we'll see any of our fairy friends today," said Rachel.

"Or any goblins," Kirsty added. "We should keep our eyes peeled – the Tippington Helper of the Year Award is being presented tomorrow and we still need to find two of the Helping Fairies' magical objects."

The nominations for the Tippington Helper of the Year Award had been announced at the start of the week. It was a very important local prize that recognised the special people in the community whose job was to help others.

Read **Perrie the Paramedic Fairy** to find out what adventures are in store for Kirsty and Rachel!

Competition!

The Helping Fairies have created a special
competition just for you!

Collect all four books in the Helping Fairies series
and answer the special questions in the back of each one.

Once you have all the answers, take the first letter from
each one and arrange them to spell a secret word!
When you have the answer, go online and enter!

What is the name of
Bailey's kitten?

— — — — — —

We will put all the correct entries into a draw and select
a winner to receive a special Rainbow Magic Goody Bag
featuring lots of treats for you and your fairy friends.
You'll also feature in a new Rainbow Magic story!

Enter online now at www.rainbowmagicbooks.co.uk

Join in the magic online by signing up
to the Rainbow Magic fan club!

Meet the fairies, play games and
get sneak peeks at the latest books!

There's fairy fun for everyone at

www.rainbowmagicbooks.co.uk

You'll find great activities, competitions, stories and
fairy profiles, and also a special newsletter.

Find a fairy with
your name!